SONIC THE HEDGEHOG™

BY

MICHAEL

TEITELBAUM

INTERIOR

ILLUSTRATIONS BY

GLEN HANSON

Troll Associates

Produced by Creative Media Applications, Inc.
Art direction by Fabia Wargin.
Cover art by Greg Wray.

This book is dedicated to Chrissy, Lauren, Dana, and Sheryl.

Special thanks to Roy Wandelmaier, Arlene Scanlan, Bob Harris, and Susan Reyes.

Prologue

Welcome to the planet Mobius.

Mobius is a dark and dreary place. It is ruled by the evil Dr. Robotnik. Robotnik's factories pour dirty smoke into the air. Schools and libraries are always closed. Music and dancing are against the law. So is playing games.

Evil robots patrol the planet. They make sure no one ever has any fun. Robotnik's law says, "If you have fun, you go to jail."

All in all, Mobius is a rotten place to live.

But it wasn't always that way.

Once, Mobius was a wonderful planet ruled by a good king. The air was clean. So were the parks and streets. Children played baseball and ate ice cream. People read books and went to the movies. Everyone had fun.

But that was all before Dr. Robotnik took over the planet.

How could such a terrible thing happen to such a wonderful place? Come back with us now to the time when all was well on the planet Mobius.

But hurry. You've got to move pretty fast to keep up with a speedy blue hedgehog named Sonic!

Chapter

1

Years ago, when things were right
on Mobius, there lived a hedgehog named
Sonic and a boy named Robotnik. Sonic The
Hedgehog was a seven-year-old orphan. He
lived with his Uncle Chuck. Robotnik was
fifteen and also an orphan. He lived with
Uncle Chuck too. Even as children, Sonic and
Robotnik did not get along.

Robotnik was only interested in building
robots. He would spend his days working with
mechanical parts in Uncle Chuck's backyard.
He wanted to build robots that would do
anything he asked.

Sonic was only interested in running as fast

as he could. Every day he practiced. At the end of most days he fell right into bed.

• • • • •

ZOOM!

Sonic streaked across his Uncle Chuck's backyard in a blue blur. He was headed for Uncle Chuck's workshop.

Sonic was a short blue hedgehog. He had sharp pointy spines. The spines ran from the top of his head all the way down his back.

Uncle Chuck looked like Sonic. Except that Uncle Chuck had bushy white eyebrows and a thick white mustache.

Uncle Chuck was a great inventor. Sonic was very proud of his uncle.

"Hey, Uncle Chuck!" said Sonic, as he stepped into the workshop. Smoke curled from the soles of Sonic's sneakers.

"Looks like you burned out another pair of sneakers," said Uncle Chuck. "You're just too fast for your own shoes!"

"You bet, Uncle Chuck," said Sonic, proud of himself.

With a *WHOOSH!* Sonic sped out of the workshop.

Uncle Chuck clicked on his stopwatch.

Trees and bushes swayed from the wind Sonic made as he zoomed around the neighborhood.

A group of children playing nearby were blown off their feet.

"What was that?" asked one of the children.

"I don't know," said another. "But it was blue. And it sure was fast."

A few seconds later Sonic returned to Uncle Chuck's workshop.

"Once around the neighborhood," said Sonic. "How did I do?"

Uncle Chuck clicked off his stopwatch. "Four point two seconds," he said. "Not bad, my boy. Not bad at all."

The smoke from Sonic's sneakers was thicker than before.

"One of these days I've got to invent a pair of special sneakers for you," said Uncle Chuck. "Sneakers that can handle your incredible speed."

"What are you working on now?" asked Sonic.

"I just finished inventing this magic power ring," said Uncle Chuck. He handed Sonic a golden ring. It glowed with a strange yellow light.

"What does it do?" asked Sonic.

"It will increase your speed and power, Sonic," explained Uncle Chuck. "But it will work only for you."

Someone called from the backyard. "Hey, Chuck! Bring me the turbo-wrench, will you?"

"Robotnik," groaned Sonic. "You know, Uncle Chuck, I think he steals parts from your

equipment. Then he uses them for his dumb little robots."

"Oh, I don't know," said Uncle Chuck. "He's all right, I guess." Uncle Chuck trusted everyone. "I'm busy working on this ring, Sonic. Would you take the turbo-wrench out to Robotnik?"

"Okay," said Sonic, scowling. "But I'm doing it for you, not for him!"

Sonic took the wrench and zipped out to the backyard in the blink of an eye.

"What took you so long, slowpoke?" asked Robotnik. He grabbed the turbo-wrench. "Give me that."

Sonic shook his head. Then he zoomed out of the backyard. He went looking for someone who was more fun to play with.

Robotnik turned back to the robot he was working on. This was the tenth robot he had built. The first nine each worked for a little while. Then they stopped. Some just blew up.

The remains of the first nine robots sat in a junk pile in a corner of the backyard. All of Robotnik's failures did not stop him from trying.

"I need steering parts for this robot," he said to himself. "Then it will be finished. Now, where can I get steering parts? Hmmm."

Robotnik spotted Uncle Chuck's tractor. "He won't miss these," said Robotnik, as he took apart the tractor. "He never uses this old thing anyway."

Robotnik removed the tractor's steering parts. Then he placed them in his robot. "Now for the big test."

He pressed a switch on his remote control. The robot sprang to life. Lights flashed. Buzzers buzzed and beepers beeped. The robot turned its head toward Robotnik.

"What-is-your-command-Master?" said the robot in a squeaky voice.

"It works!" cried Robotnik. "Ha! Ha! Robot,

go to that pile of junk and bring me all the old robot heads."

"Yes-Master," said the robot. It took two steps, then stopped. The robot pulled its own head off. Then it rolled its head on the ground like a bowling ball.

"No!" cried Robotnik. "That's wrong!" He sat on the ground and threw a tantrum. "They never work! Never! Never! Never!"

After a few minutes Robotnik calmed down. He picked up the robot's head and began to put it back on.

•••••

Back in his workshop, Uncle Chuck remembered something. He had promised to lend his tractor to a neighbor. He went outside, climbed aboard the old tractor, and started it up.

The tractor rolled wildly around the backyard. Uncle Chuck tried to steer it, but he couldn't control it. It would not respond.

"I don't understand," he cried. "Why can't I steer this tractor?"

When he looked up, Uncle Chuck saw that the tractor was headed right for Robotnik!

Chapter
2

"Look out!" cried Uncle Chuck.

But he was too late. With a loud crash, the tractor smashed right into Robotnik and his newest robot.

Robot arms and legs flew into the air. The robot's head landed in the junk pile. Robotnik and Uncle Chuck ended up between the tractor and a tree. They were trapped.

"You crazy old fool!" shouted Robotnik. "What's the idea of driving this tractor right into me?"

"I don't know what went wrong," said Uncle Chuck. "I couldn't control the steering!"

"You're just a dumb old man, that's all!" snarled Robotnik. "How are we going to move this thing and get free?"

• • • • •

Not far away, Sonic was playing baseball with some friends. Nine kids played on one team. Sonic played by himself against them.

"Batter up!" said Sonic. He stood on the pitcher's mound. Sonic threw a pitch. Then he ran to home plate faster than the ball. He was waiting there to catch it when the batter swung and missed.

"Strike one!" shouted Sonic.

Back on the pitcher's mound, he threw the next pitch and ran to the plate. This time, the batter hit the ball toward second base. No one was playing the field.

Sonic took off! He arrived at second base in time to field the ball. Then he threw it toward first base. Sonic zoomed to first base and caught the ball. The runner was out!

"You're too fast for us, Sonic," said a kid on the other team. "Even if you are the only guy on your team!"

Suddenly, Sonic heard a cry for help. It came from Uncle Chuck's workshop.

"Sorry, guys, I have to go," said Sonic. "We'll finish the game later."

WHOOSH!

Sonic took off in a blue blur. Within seconds he arrived at the workshop.

"Uncle Chuck!" he cried, spotting his uncle and Robotnik trapped by the tractor. "What happened?"

"Never mind that now!" shouted Robotnik. "Just get us out of here!"

"I'll try," said Sonic. He pushed the tractor with all his might. "It's too heavy. I can't budge it."

Then Sonic remembered Uncle Chuck's magic power ring. "Wait here," he said.

"Where do you think we're going?" snapped Robotnik. "On a picnic?"

Sonic dashed into the workshop. He grabbed the magic ring and ran back outside. By the time Sonic reached the tractor, he was glowing with a bright yellow light.

Sonic felt amazingly strong. He lifted the tractor with just one hand. Uncle Chuck and Robotnik were free.

"I'd better get you two to the hospital," said Sonic. "Just to be on the safe side."

Sonic still glowed all over with yellow from the ring. He felt very powerful and very fast. He picked up Uncle Chuck and Robotnik, one in each arm. "Hold tight. Here we go."

Sonic sped off toward the hospital, carrying Uncle Chuck and Robotnik with ease.

Chapter
3

Uncle Chuck and Robotnik were looked over at the hospital. They were sent home the very same day.

"Thanks to your bravery and speed, Sonic, we're fine," said Uncle Chuck.

"And thanks to your stupid tractor, we got into this mess in the first place," said Robotnik. He stormed off to be alone.

•••••

Back at the workshop, Sonic watched as Uncle Chuck created more magic power rings. Robotnik was out in the backyard. He was trying to build another robot.

There was a knock on the workshop door.

"Come in," said Uncle Chuck.

The door opened. Standing there was one of Robotnik's first robots. It looked like a giant tin can. It had old drainpipes for arms and legs. It had a toaster for a head. One leg was shorter than the other. Steam poured from its ears as it spoke.

"Excuse me, Mr. Uncle Chuck," said the robot. "May I speak with you?"

"Of course," said Uncle Chuck. "Come in."

"If Mr. Robotnik knew I was here, he'd be very upset, sir," said the robot. "But I just had to tell you."

"Tell me what?" asked Uncle Chuck.

"Well, sir," began the robot. "In order to make his robots, Mr. Robotnik has been taking parts from your machinery. Look closely at my body. I'm made from the hood of your truck."

"I wondered where that went," said Uncle Chuck, scratching his head.

"Most recently, sir," continued the robot, "Mr. Robotnik took the steering parts out of your tractor. He put them into his latest robot."

"I knew it!" said Sonic.

"So Robotnik was responsible for our accident," said Uncle Chuck. Now he was getting angry. "And he blamed me!"

Uncle Chuck stormed from his workshop into the backyard.

"What do *you* want?" asked Robotnik.

"Young man," said Uncle Chuck. "You are grounded for taking my tractor's steering parts, and then lying to me. Go to your room and stay there!"

Robotnik grumbled. Then he picked up his tools and went to his room.

●●●●●

Over the next few weeks Sonic and Uncle Chuck spent their time in the workshop. They were working on the magic rings.

Robotnik spent his time inside the house. He was stealing parts from every household appliance he could find. His room was filled with blenders, microwaves, answering machines, CD players, and more. He took these apart and built his strangest creation yet.

One afternoon, Sonic and Uncle Chuck were in the workshop. They heard a loud crash outside.

"What was that?" asked Uncle Chuck.

"I don't know," said Sonic. "But I'll bet Robotnik has something to do with it."

Sonic and Uncle Chuck raced toward the house. In the backyard, they stopped short. Standing in front of them was a giant mechanical monster. The front door to the house was shattered. The monster had smashed its way out.

Robotnik stood a few feet away from the monster, holding a remote control.

"I'm through with you!" Robotnik snarled at

Uncle Chuck. Then he pressed a button on the remote.

The monster grabbed Uncle Chuck and lifted him into the air. "Run for cover, Sonic!" cried Uncle Chuck.

"I'll do better than that," said Sonic. "I'll save you from Robotnik's monster, and we won't have to run anywhere!"

Sonic raced to the garden hose. He grabbed one end. Using his super speed, Sonic ran around the monster again and again.

When Sonic was finished, the monster was completely tied up with the hose. It tried to take a step, but it tripped and crashed to the ground.

"It looks like your monster is going to be tied up for a while, Robotnik," said Sonic.

As the monster fell, Uncle Chuck went flying from its arms. Sonic caught Uncle Chuck just before he hit the ground.

Robotnik kneeled over his fallen robot. He looked up at Sonic and Uncle Chuck. "You two have ruined my robots for the last time," he said. "I'm out of here. But I'll get you back. Just you wait and see!"

Chapter
4

Eight years passed.

No one had heard from Robotnik since the day he left.

Sonic grew up. He was now a happy fifteen-year-old. He was even faster than he had been as a young hedgehog. Uncle Chuck bought Sonic a dog named Muttski. They were best friends.

Uncle Chuck continued to invent things. He had also opened a food stand called Chuck's Chili Dogs. The chili-dog stand was set up right next to his workshop. Sonic worked as the delivery boy for his Uncle Chuck.

One day Uncle Chuck was in the chili-dog stand waiting for Sonic to return from a delivery. Uncle Chuck was very excited about his latest invention. *I can't wait until Sonic gets back and sees what I've made for him,* thought Uncle Chuck.

A few minutes later Sonic zoomed up to the stand. "I'm back," he said. "But I've ruined another pair of sneakers." The soles of Sonic's sneakers were smoking, as usual.

Uncle Chuck was bursting with excitement. "I'm so glad you're back!" he said.

He handed Sonic a pair of brand-new bright red sneakers. "Try these on!" said Uncle Chuck. "I made them from a special material. They won't burn up, even when you're traveling at top speed!"

Sonic put on the sneakers. "Way cool!" he said. "They fit perfectly. Let me take them out for a spin. A Sonic spin!"

"Here," said Uncle Chuck, handing Sonic a

bag full of chili dogs. "Try them out while you make this delivery."

Sonic disappeared in a blue and red blur. A few seconds later, he returned.

"Wow!" said Uncle Chuck. "Record time!"

"These new sneakers are beyond excellent," said Sonic. "Look, no smoke!"

The phone in the chili-dog stand rang. Uncle Chuck picked it up.

"Chuck's Chili Dogs, Chuck speaking," he said. "What . . . how many? Er . . . no problem. Sure, we can deliver them. You'll have them in no time. Thanks!" He hung up the phone and grinned.

"Big order?" asked Sonic.

"The biggest ever!" said Uncle Chuck. "Two hundred chili dogs!"

"Two hundred!" said Sonic. "Wow! Let's get busy!"

They went to work. Uncle Chuck made the

chili dogs. Sonic piled them into a wheelbarrow.

"That's the last one," said Uncle Chuck.
Sonic placed it on top of the huge pile. "Take it away, Sonic!"

"I'll be back before you know it," said Sonic.
"Stand back, I'm making tracks."

Sonic lifted the wheelbarrow's handles and took off in a flash.

"Look at him go, Muttski," said Uncle
Chuck. Muttski wagged his tail. "It's great to get such a big order!"

Uncle Chuck was so glad he laughed and did a little dance. Muttski barked happily.

Then a change came over Muttski. He began to growl at something behind Uncle Chuck.

"What's the matter, boy?" asked Uncle
Chuck. When he turned around he saw five huge robots.

"What's going on here?" asked Uncle Chuck.
"Who are you?"

A familiar figure stepped out from behind the robots. It was Robotnik!

"Perhaps you recognize me!" he said.

"Robotnik!" cried Uncle Chuck. "I recognize your voice now. You ordered the 200 chili dogs. What are you up to? What's going on?"

"I'll let my swatbots explain," said Robotnik.

"You-were-laughing-and-dancing," said one of the robots. "That-is-now-illegal. You-are-under-arrest."

"What? Says who?" asked Uncle Chuck.

"Says me," replied Robotnik. "I've declared myself the new King of Mobius. I have made laws against singing, dancing, reading, laughing, and having any fun. And my team of swatbots are enforcing my new laws!"

Two swatbots grabbed Uncle Chuck and Muttski. "You two, take them away!" ordered Robotnik. "The rest of you, destroy this place!"

Uncle Chuck tried to kick his way free. But he couldn't break loose from the swatbot's grasp. Muttski growled, trying to free himself. They were dragged off by the swatbots.

A terrible thought crossed Uncle Chuck's mind. *If Robotnik ordered the chili dogs, then Sonic must be walking into a trap!*

Chapter
5

Sonic zoomed along the road at top speed. He pushed the wheelbarrow full of chili dogs in front of him.

These new sneakers sure feel great, he thought.

He soon arrived at the address where the chili dogs were supposed to be delivered.

What an awful-looking place, thought Sonic. He was standing in front of a dirty, run-down factory. The factory's chimney poured thick smoke into the air.

It really stinks here, thought Sonic. *I'll make this a fast delivery and motor out of here!*

Sonic knocked on the factory's metal door. A

robot that looked like a chicken answered.

"What-do-you-want?" it asked.

"Chili-dog delivery," said Sonic.

"Come-in," said the robot. Then it disappeared down a dark hallway.

Sonic stepped inside. He heard a deep rumbling from above. He looked up just in time to see a huge metal ball fall from the ceiling.

Sonic used all his speed to dash out of the way. The ball crashed down on the wheelbarrow. The chili dogs splattered all over.

"Oh, great," said Sonic. "There goes Uncle Chuck's all-time biggest order."

Suddenly, ten mechanical arms popped out of the walls. Each one was holding a hammer.

"Yikes!" shouted Sonic. "Gotta juice!"

Sonic sped along the hallway. One by one the arms came down. The hammers smashed on the ground. Each one narrowly missed Sonic.

Something here is ultra uncool, thought Sonic. *This whole factory is one big booby trap. Whoever ordered those chili dogs wanted to trap me here.*

Then a terrible thought crossed Sonic's mind. *Whoever wanted to trap me here might be after Uncle Chuck! He could be in big trouble. Time to go!*

At that moment a team of swatbots came stomping down the hallway.

"Halt-hedgehog!" ordered one of the swatbots.

"No way, robot dude," said Sonic. "I'm out of here!"

Sonic sped down the hallway and out the front door. He left the swatbots in his dust.

Sonic arrived at the chili-dog stand a few seconds later. His mouth opened in horror.

"The stand!" cried Sonic. "It's been smashed to bits." Sonic zoomed to the workshop.

"Uncle Chuck! Muttski!" he called out. "Oh, no, they're gone!"

"You-are-under-arrest-hedgehog!" a voice boomed from behind Sonic.

Sonic turned around. He was face to face with another team of swatbots.

Sonic charged at the lead swatbot and leaped right onto its head. "Where have you taken Uncle Chuck and Muttski, you walking junk pile!" demanded Sonic.

"Destroy-the-hedgehog!" ordered the swatbot.

"Oh, really?" said Sonic. "I think I'll do the destroying instead!"

Sonic whirled into a Super Sonic Spin. He rolled into a ball, then spun faster and faster. He became a round blue blur.

CRASH! Sonic smashed into the swatbots. He bounced from one to another like a pinball hitting bumpers in a pinball machine. His hedgehog spines cut through the evil robots like buzz-saw blades.

The smoke cleared. Swatbot pieces were

scattered all over. Sonic picked up one of the pieces and read some writing on it.

"Made by Robotnik, new King of Mobius," Sonic read aloud. "Robotnik! So that's what he's been up to. That must have been his factory I was in. He's got Uncle Chuck and Muttski. But not for long! Sonic The Hedgehog is on his way!"

VA-ROOM! Sonic took off to Robotnik's factory.

Chapter

6

Sonic stopped in the woods just outside Robotnik's factory. He could see the tops of the chimneys pouring dirty smoke into the air. He thought about Uncle Chuck and Muttski.

"Robotnik picked the wrong hedgehog to mess with," said Sonic. "I'm heading straight in there. And when I'm through, there won't be a robot left standing."

"I wouldn't do that if I were you," said a voice from behind Sonic.

Startled, he jumped ten feet into the air. He landed, ready to smash a robot. Instead, he found himself face to face with a cute little

chipmunk girl. Her brown hair was in a ponytail.

"What's the idea of sneaking up on someone like that?" asked Sonic.

"I was only stopping you from making a big mistake," said the girl. "If you went in the front gate, the swatbots would have captured you in no time."

"Who are you?" asked Sonic.

"I'm Princess Sally Acorn," she said.

"Princess?" asked Sonic. "What's a princess doing here?"

"My father, the real King of Mobius, has been kidnapped by Robotnik," explained Sally.

"So has my uncle and my dog," said Sonic.

"And so have most of the people of Mobius," replied Sally.

"But why?" asked Sonic.

"Robotnik's taken over the planet," said Sally. "He's outlawed fun, learning, and clean air. He wants to turn Mobius into a filthy planet of robot slaves.

"Each prisoner he captures is sent through a machine called the Ro-Bo-Machine, and turned into a robot. I only hope we're in time to rescue my father and your uncle and dog. Robotnik will turn them into robots too."

"I'm going to stop him right now!" said Sonic.

"Wait, get down!" cried Sally. She grabbed Sonic's hand and pulled him to the ground.

"What the—" said Sonic.

"Shh," said Sally. "Look up there!"

Sonic saw a group of flying robots that looked like giant bumblebees.

"Those are Robotnik's buzzbombers," explained Sally. "They patrol the area around his factory. They'll pass in a minute, and then we can make our move."

When the buzzbombers had flown past, Sally and Sonic got to their feet.

"I know a short cut that will lead us right to Robotnik's Ro-Bo-Machine," said Sally. "Come on, we'll have to move fast."

Sonic smiled. "That's what I do best," he said.

Sonic blew past Sally and zoomed on ahead. Sally was startled. She had always thought of herself as a fast runner. But this blue hedgehog was amazingly quick.

Sally stood with her arms crossed. She tapped her foot impatiently.

A few seconds later Sonic returned. "Sorry. I guess I should let you go first. You're the one who knows the short cut!" said Sonic.

"I was wondering how long it would take you to figure that out!" said Sally, with a smile. "If you can slow down just a bit, I might be able to keep up with you."

"Lead on, Princess," said Sonic.

"Call me Sally," she said. "And by the way, who are you?"

"Call me Sonic," he replied. "Sonic The Hedgehog. The fastest person in all of Mobius. Pleased to meet you."

Sally nodded, then led the way. Sonic followed close behind at half speed.

Chapter
7

Sonic and Sally made their way through the woods.

"I only hope we're in time," said Sally. "I couldn't bear the thought of my father being turned into a robot."

"If Robotnik has laid one finger on Uncle Chuck or Muttski, he's going to have one hopping-mad hedgehog on his hands," added Sonic.

They soon came to a clearing. On the other side of the clearing was a large chain-link fence. Through the fence they saw a huge machine.

"That's Robotnik's Ro-Bo-Machine," said Sally.

Sonic and Sally spotted a group of people stumbling out of the machine. They walked stiffly. Their eyes were dull.

"Let's get a closer look," said Sonic.

They crossed the clearing and peered through the fence. More people stepped out of the machine. They all had that same empty look in their eyes.

"Robotnik's swatbots kidnap people," explained Sally. "He puts the people into his Ro-Bo-Machine and turns them into robots. Then he puts them to work in his factories."

"There's Robotnik now!" said Sonic.

It had been eight years since Sonic had last seen Robotnik. Robotnik's body was now bigger and uglier than ever. It seemed to overflow with evil. His oval head came to a point. He had a big, bushy mustache.

He growled at the newly made robots. Sonic and Sally could hear every word.

"Welcome to my factory, slaves," barked Robotnik.

"Thank-you-Master-Robotnik," the group said together. They spoke with hollow voices.

"Will you obey me?" asked Robotnik.

"Yes-Master-Robotnik," said the robots. "We-promise-to-work-as-your-slaves-for-the-rest-of-our-lives-oh-great-one."

"Good," snarled Robotnik. "Now, you will all go to the factory. You will work twenty-three hours a day, seven days a week. But I'm a kind and caring ruler. Each day you'll get a half hour for lunch and a half hour to sleep."

"Oh-thank-you-kind-caring-Master-Robotnik," said the robot slaves.

Sonic gasped. "Oh, no! There's Uncle Chuck and Muttski. We're too late, Sally. They've already been changed into robots."

"I'm sorry, Sonic," said Sally.

"I've got to save them," said Sonic.

"You can't help them now," said Sally.

"Ready!" shouted Robotnik. "March!"

The group of robots began to walk forward. They moved like zombies toward the factory.

"Uncle Chuck!" shouted Sonic, leaping over the fence.

"Sonic, wait!" called Sally. But it was too late.

Chapter
8

Sonic ran to Uncle Chuck and Muttski.

"Uncle Chuck, it's me, Sonic! Speak to me!"

"We-live-to-serve-Robotnik," said Uncle Chuck.

"It's really true!" cried Sonic. "He has turned you into a robot." Sonic turned to Muttski. "How about you, Muttski? Do you remember me, boy?"

"Ro-BARK-nik!" growled Muttski.

"Oh, Muttski," said Sonic, sadly. "He's changed even you."

"Well, well," said Robotnik. "Look what we have here. Another hedgehog to add to my collection. Swatbots, grab him!"

Five swatbots appeared. They grabbed Sonic.

"Put him down!" yelled Sally as she scrambled over the fence.

"This is getting better all the time," said Robotnik. "Now we have the princess as well. Seize her!"

A swatbot lifted Sally off the ground.

"Swatbots, take them to the machine at once," he ordered. "Don't worry. In a few minutes you two will be happy to be my slaves! And soon, I will do the same thing to every living being left on Mobius. Nothing but my robots will exist on this planet! And I, Robotnik, will be the supreme ruler of all!"

"No," shouted Sally, as she struggled to free herself. "Sonic, help! Don't let him turn us into machines."

"No way, Sally," said Sonic. "It's time for some super sensational Sonic swatbot smashing!"

Sonic pulled his magical power ring out of his pocket, where he had placed it earlier. The

ring filled him with super Sonic power and speed. He whipped into a Super Sonic Spin, breaking free of the swatbots' grasps. Then he smashed into one swatbot after another like a swirling blue tornado.

The swatbot that held Sally put her down. It turned toward Sonic. He smashed the robot to pieces.

One by one, Sonic destroyed the swatbots with his Super Sonic Spin. Then he ran to Uncle Chuck and Muttski.

"Uncle Chuck! Muttski!" said Sonic. "Come on, let's go!"

But Uncle Chuck and Muttski didn't move. They stared straight ahead.

"Sally," called Sonic. "You carry Muttski. I'll pick up Uncle Chuck. We've got to get them out of here."

Sonic placed Uncle Chuck gently across his shoulders. Sally held Muttski in her arms.

Sonic and Sally climbed over the fence,

carrying their rescued prisoners. They ran from the factory. Far behind them, they could hear Robotnik screaming in anger.

"I'm sorry we didn't find your father, Sally," said Sonic.

"Me too," said Sally, sadly. "But our fight with Robotnik is not over. In fact it's just begun."

"What do you mean?" asked Sonic.

"I'd like to share a secret with you," said Sally. "I want you to meet some friends of mine. Let's head for the Great Forest."

"The Great Forest?" said Sonic. "But there's no one living there."

"Yes there is, Sonic," said Sally, smiling. "I'll explain along the way."

Chapter
9

Sally and Sonic headed to the Great Forest of Mobius. They carried Uncle Chuck and Muttski. On the way, Sally shared her secret.

"When Robotnik took over Mobius and kidnapped my father, a small group of us decided to fight back," she explained. "We call ourselves Freedom Fighters. We want to turn Mobius back to the way it was before. We'll do anything to get rid of Robotnik."

"You all hide in the forest?" asked Sonic.

"Yes."

"Why doesn't Robotnik know you're living in the Great Forest?" asked Sonic.

"We live in a secret underground town called Knothole Village. It's under the forest floor," said Sally.

"That's amazing," said Sonic. "But why are you telling me all this?"

"We could use your help," said Sally. "Would you join us?"

"You bet!" said Sonic. "Robotnik destroyed my home and turned my family into robots. I'd do anything to stop him. It would be way cool to be one of your Freedom Fighters. I'm always glad to help when my speed is in need!"

"I like your style, Sonic," said Sally. "Welcome to our group."

After some time, they reached the Great Forest. Sally led the way into the forest. They soon came to a large tree stump.

"This is the secret entrance to Knothole Village," said Sally, pointing at the stump. "Here, give me a hand."

Sonic helped Sally lift the top off the stump. They slipped inside, then let the top close behind them.

Sonic followed Sally down a winding slide which took them along the hidden passageway to Knothole Village. When they reached the bottom, Sally put Muttski down, and Sonic sat Uncle Chuck in a chair.

Sally introduced Sonic to her group. "This is my new friend, Sonic The Hedgehog," she said. "He's joining our team."

Everyone welcomed Sonic.

"What are we going to do about your uncle and your dog?" asked Sally. "They're still robot-a-cized."

"Good point," said Sonic. "Hey! Maybe this will help." Sonic pulled out his power ring.

The whole room filled with bright yellow light. Uncle Chuck and Muttski began to glow.

When the glowing stopped, they were back to normal.

"Sonic!" cried Uncle Chuck. "What happened? Where are we?"

Muttski whimpered and rubbed his nose against Sonic.

Sonic petted Muttski as he filled Uncle Chuck in on the day's exciting events.

"That means we can use Sonic's power rings to restore Robotnik's other prisoners," said Uncle Chuck.

"This gives me a lot of hope for my father and the others, Sonic," said Sally. "I'm glad you're now a Freedom Fighter!"

Sonic was happy. He was certain now that, with the help of the Freedom Fighters and his power rings, he would be able to defeat Robotnik and restore the King of Mobius to his rightful place on the throne.

Mobius would once again be a great place to live. A place where songs were sung and books were read. A place where having fun was the most important thing anyone could do!